The Look Outs and
the Stolen Puppies

The Look Outs and the Stolen Puppies

E. R. Reilly

© E.R. Reilly, 2010

Published by   Santiago Press
                PO Box 8808
                Birmingham
                B30 2LR

Email for orders and enquiries:
santiago@reilly19.freesereve.co.uk

Illustrations © Kay Loxley, 2010

ISBN 978-0-9562568-1-2

Reprinted - 2012.

Printed and bound in India by Authentic Media
A division of OM Books Foundation, Secunderabad 500 067, India
E-mail: printing@ombooks.org

Chapter One – The Stolen Puppies

There's something that you need to know about me; I steal things. I know I shouldn't and I really am going to stop doing it. I don't know why I do it. Well, I do really; I just like it. I'll steal something in this story. I'm not going to keep going on about it except to say I know it's wrong and I really am going to stop doing it. The surprising thing about me stealing things is that I should know better, you see. I'm a detective. I'm a member of a detective club called The Look Outs.

We used to be three ordinary children doing the things that all children do and we just happened to live in the same block of flats. That was until we saw a burglar. We all agreed that we couldn't let the burglar get away with his crime, so we decided to form our own detective agency and track him down. You are probably wondering why we didn't just tell the police. Well, we couldn't you see. When we saw the burglar, we were actually stealing something ourselves. We were scrumping. That's what you call it when you steal apples from a tree. Sometimes, on our way home from school, I climbed over a garden wall and picked three apples off a tree and Marion and Mark kept a look out to make sure that nobody was coming. That's what we were doing when we saw a man dressed in black jump over a wall and run off. He was wearing a hoody and he had something under his arm. When we found out that an expensive painting had been stolen, we knew he must have been the burglar, but we also knew that if we went to the police, they would find out that we had been stealing apples. So, it was then that we decided to form our detective agency and call it The Look Outs.

The case of the stolen painting was our first case and we successfully tracked down the burglar by following every single clue that we could find. That was quite some time ago and since then, we have been trying to find a new case to solve. One morning, we woke up as normal, but before we had got to school, we knew exactly what our next case was going to be.

Everybody was talking about one thing and one thing only. Seven pedigree dogs had been stolen. They were Golden Retrievers and they were only puppies. They were only four or five weeks old so they were too young to even be away from their mother. The puppies were stolen from a house at the bottom of our estate.

We live in a block of flats. I'm Peter and the other two Look Outs are Marion and Mark. We walked to school with Marion's mum and Mark's kind-of step mum. We never talked about the stolen puppies on the way to school because we only ever discuss Look Outs business in private. When we got to school, everybody there was talking about the stolen puppies. People were saying that the puppies could be worth hundreds or even thousands of pounds.

Our teacher is a nun. Her name is Sister Bernadeen. We said prayers for the missing puppies in assembly and Sister Bernadeen said that we should all pray for their safe return. It was really sad to think of the little puppies being frightened and not knowing what was going to happen to them. When we were saying a prayer for the safe return of the puppies, I looked across to Mark and Marion. Mark rubbed his ear and Marion rubbed hers. Then I rubbed mine. That was one of our secret signs. It meant it was time for us to hold a secret meeting. We all knew that we would find an excuse to talk privately as soon as we could.

During the first lesson, Marion went to the bin at the front of the class to sharpen her pencil. She looked round to me and Mark and nodded her head for us to come as well. Mark and I quietly made our way to the bin whilst everybody else carried on working. Marion said that we should meet up as soon as possible to decide if we were going to make the missing puppies our next case. Mark said, "Of course we are" and I agreed. Marion said that we needed to meet up as soon as possible to make plans. Sister Bernadeen called across the room to ask what the three of us were up to. Marion called out, "Nothing Sister". I said in a really low whisper that we should meet up at dinnertime, but Marion said that she couldn't get out of guitar club. Sister Bernadeen said, "Come along, you three. Get on with your work now."

As we were walking back to our desks, Mark said, "In the den. As soon as we get home." We could see that Sister Bernadeen was looking at us, so we just nodded and went back to our seats. It was decided then. The next official meeting of The Look Outs would be held in the den as soon as we could possibly get to it after we got home. I loved our first adventure so much, I couldn't wait for the new one to begin. I can't stand waiting for good things to happen. That day at school was the longest school day in years. I couldn't concentrate on anything because all I could think about was our new adventure. If it turned out to be half as much fun as the first one, we were in for a real treat.

I told you that we live in a block of flats. Well, I live on the ground floor and Marion and Mark live upstairs. Marion's flat is directly above mine. Mark lives with his dad and his little brother. He also lives with his dad's new partner. She's not really his step mum, but she acts like she is. So we call her his kind-of step mum. She's really strict. She's always telling him to do jobs, like tidy his room. I don't go to his house much because his kind-of step mum is so strict, but also because his dad works shifts. That means that his dad is quite often trying to sleep when everybody else is awake. His dad is a policeman which comes in handy because we can get information out of him that isn't known to the general public. He wouldn't tell us anything if he knew we were going to use it for detective work, so we have to be really careful about how we ask him stuff. We have to pretend to show an interest in his work and he likes that so that's how we get away with it.

Marion lives with her mum and dad. She's got a brother and a sister, but they're both grown up and quite old. Her parents are really old. They're about forty or fifty, I think, or something like that. I live with my dad. I don't get to see him as often as I would like to. He works every day then he goes to the pub in the evenings. My mum died when I was a baby. I don't get told what to do much. I can go out when I want to and come home when I want to. I'm pretty sure that Mark's kind-of step mum tells my dad pretty much everything that I do though. I do get a bit lonely at times, but I spend as much time as I can with Marion and Mark. Sometimes, I go to Marion's flat and I do occasionally go to Mark's flat as well, but most of the time, we meet up in our den.

You should see our den. There's a row of sheds on the ground floor of our flats. One of them is our den. It's the best one because it has a window in it and it has a light. There's a settee in there and a ledge. Two of us can fit on the settee and the other one sits on the ledge. We're supposed to take it in turns to sit on the ledge, but normally, the first two to arrive sit on the settee and the third one sits on the ledge. Everything to do with The Look Outs is strictly secret. We don't tell anybody anything about Look Outs business.

I told you that we have a secret sign to say that we need to talk in private. That's what rubbing our ears means. If we say the word 'apples', that means that we need to have a Look Outs meeting in the den. If we say the word 'sausages' when we are on the phone, it means that somebody is listening to us, so we can't speak freely. We sometimes write the word 'sausages' if somebody is looking at what we are writing on the computer.

We met up as soon as we could after we got home from school. I went straight there, because I don't need to get permission to go. Once

Marion and Mark were allowed out, they joined me. Marion brought a notebook with her. She always does. I don't think that we could ever be a real detective agency if it were not for Marion. She makes us do everything properly. She makes us log every little clue. That's really important because when you are investigating a crime, you never know when a tiny clue may turn out to be really important. You never know. That's why you have to be really careful. Me and Mark probably wouldn't be so careful if it weren't for Marion making us.

As soon as we were all together, Marion told us that we should begin by saying everything that we know about the missing dogs. We just sort of stared at each other for a second or two. The truth is that we knew very little. We knew where the dogs lived and we knew that seven puppies had been stolen during last night and that was it. Marion said that we needed to establish as many facts as we could before we could even think about tracking down the thieves. We spent some time talking about the different things that we could do and we came up with this list:

a) We needed to talk to the owners of the puppies so that we could establish the facts properly and not just rely on hearsay.

b) We needed to find out if anybody in the area saw or heard anything that may be of some use to us.

c) We needed to collect as much photographic evidence as quickly as we could.

We all agreed that there was no time to lose. We needed to find these things out today if possible, before the trail went cold.

It was easy for me, I could go and start work straight away, but Marion and Mark needed to get permission. We all knew that it would be really hard for them to get permission. Their parents don't just allow them to go out for any old reason. They have to have a really good excuse.

Mark and I know that Marion is the really clever one in the Look Outs and even Mark knows himself that he's not really clever all of the time, but I'll say this for Mark, he comes up with some fantastic ideas sometimes. He suggested that he and Marion should tell their parents that their homework was to do some research about the stolen puppies for the school newspaper. Marion and I thought that was a really super idea and we decided straight away that that was exactly what they should do.

I waited in the den and the other two ran upstairs to try and get permission to go and do our research. Marion got permission and came back downstairs in no time. She had her phone in her hand ready to take all of the photographs that we needed.

Mark came down a few minutes later, but he wasn't very happy. His kind-of step mum said that it was nearly time for his tea so he couldn't go. He said that he would be allowed to do some research when he came home from school tomorrow before his tea. We agreed that we would do

what we could tonight and that we would have another meeting of The Look Outs on the next day where we would make notes of everything that we have already found out and then finish off any research that we hadn't already finished.

Marion said that she would take as many photographs of the scene as she could and that I should go and talk to the owners of the dogs. There are four blocks of flats on our estate and there's a road that runs along the side of it. There are a row of houses all along the side of the road and the puppies were stolen from one of the houses. I knew the people who lived there, so it was no problem for me to go and talk to them.

We ran down the road to where the house was and I knocked on the door. Marion went around to the back of the house to start taking photographs. There was an entry which led to the back of the houses.

Each of the houses had a small garden. Behind the gardens was an alleyway that was wide enough for people to walk up and down, but it was too narrow to drive a car down. On the other side of the alleyway was a large wooden fence with even larger trees on the other side of that. On the other side of the fence were the grounds to the old folks' home. Nuns live there. They look after the old folks. It's sometimes called a convent because that's what you call a place where nuns live. Our teacher, Sister Bernadeen lives there.

Marion took photographs of absolutely everything. She took

photographs of every centimetre of the ground outside of the garden. So if there were any footprints or if the thieves left any clues whatsoever, then we would have photographic evidence to refer to.

I knew that there were two teenage boys in the house because they used to come to our school. One of them came to the door and I told him I was writing a report for the school newspaper and I asked him if I could question him about the theft of the puppies. He told me that he was happy to answer any questions that I had because he wanted as much publicity as possible. The interview was really good. He told me every last detail and I promised him that I would make sure

that everybody who read the school newspaper would get to know all of the details.

Marion and I ran all the way back to the den. When we got there, she showed me the pictures. There were some good shots of footprints, but

nothing else seemed to be of much help. The thing with clues is that you never know whether something very small, like a little piece of material, might turn out to be a really important clue. It was a little piece of material that helped us to catch the burglar in our first case.

I found out that the puppies had been put in the shed at the bottom of the garden because they were making too much noise in the night and upsetting the other dogs in the house. We agreed that whoever took them must have parked a car up nearby. They couldn't have climbed over the fence because it would have made too much noise. We agreed that the thieves must have parked the car somewhere nearby and crept up on the puppies in the shed.

Marion got a text from her mum saying that it was time for her to go home. We decided that we would tell Mark everything on the way to school in the morning, if we could do it without being overheard and then have another Look Outs meeting in the den after school.

Marion went upstairs to her flat and I went into mine. My dad had left me some tea to warm up in the microwave. I don't really get lonely that much, but when Marion and Mark go home to their families and I go home to an empty flat, well that first few minutes when I'm on my own can be a bit sad, but it doesn't last too long. I watched a bit of telly and went to bed.

On the way to school in the morning, we told Mark everything that had happened the night before.

He said that he would interview other neighbours to see if they saw or heard anything. He asked his kind-of step mum if he could do it after school. He said it was so he could write a piece for the school newspaper. The good news was that his kind-of step mum said, "Yes", but she also said that she would go along with him to keep an eye on him. That was alright, so long as we got all of the information that we needed, it didn't matter how we got it. We agreed that Marion would try and read Sister Bernadeen's newspaper and Mark and I would get onto the

Internet and we would all try to find out as much news about the missing puppies as we could. We met up in the den after tea to share everything that we knew.

There was nothing for me to share from the Internet and there was no mention of the puppies at all in the newspaper. Mark had been a star though. He came up with something really good in his door-to-door enquiries. He told us that one of the neighbours had seen a car roll up close to the house without its engine running. She thought that it had just broken down at the time and she thought no more of it. This was really excellent news, because it fell in nicely with the idea that Marion and I had about the thieves approaching the puppies silently.

That was good, but the other thing that Mark did was brilliant. He sneaked up on his dad when his dad was having a snooze and looked through his notebook. His dad had made some notes about the puppies. The police took the reports of some sightings seriously. Some people had said that they had seen some puppies in the back of a car near the Lickey Hills. That was only about a mile from where the puppies were stolen. Mark's dad had made a note saying that the puppies were likely to be stolen by somebody who lives locally and that they would need somewhere quiet to keep the puppies away from people who could hear them barking.

I really felt that we had enough information to have a good chance of catching the thieves. Mark was really funny; he told us that he crawled into the living room on this hands and knees when his dad was snoozing on the settee. He said his dad went quiet and he just froze still until his dad started to snore again. Then he sat behind the chair reading his notebook and once he found out the stuff about the puppies, he slipped the book back into his dad's pocket and crept out of the room. His dad woke up and asked him why he was crawling around on his hand and knees. Mark said that he thought he had seen a spider and Mark's dad seemed satisfied with that and went back to sleep.

Marion was busy writing all of the time whilst Mark was telling his story. We asked her what on earth she was making so many notes about.

It turned out that she was writing a report about the missing puppies for the school magazine. I told you that Marion worked really hard, didn't I? It was a good idea to write a report for the school newspaper, because that will allow us to use the same excuse next time we wanted to go exploring. It was a good idea because the report would make people listen out for the puppies. It also reminded us that we should be searching for the puppies somewhere locally and somewhere in a quiet place where people wouldn't hear the puppies barking.

Chapter Two – The Missing Man

The search for the stolen puppies was enough to keep us busy for every spare moment that we could find for The Look Outs, but something else happened that was just too important for us to ignore.

We heard on the news that a man had gone missing and he was a man who lived in our parish. When we got to school that morning we gave each other the secret signs which meant that we had to talk about Look Outs business. When we were supposed to be working in class, we each got up and went over to the bin in the corner of the room and pretended to sharpen our pencils. We had

 all heard the news about the missing man and we all knew that it was too important

to leave alone. It was exactly the kind of thing that The Look Outs should investigate. We quickly agreed that we should keep trying to find out who stole the Golden Retriever puppies, but that we should also try to solve the case of the missing man. Sister Bernadeen asked us what was taking so long and we all said, "Nothing Sister" and we walked back to our desks but as we went back, we agreed in a whisper that we would hold a meeting of The Look Outs as soon as we got home from school.

The rest of that day seemed to take forever. Time always seemed to pass really slowly when you were looking forward to something, but eventually the end of the school day came and we raced home. I went straight to the den because there's nobody in when I get home. So that means that I don't have somebody telling me what to do all of the time. Marion's mum is quite strict and Mark's kind-of step mum is very strict, but they both managed to join me in the den and we started a new meeting of The Look Outs in no time at all.

Marion got her note pad out and started taking notes. The first thing that we said was that we were definitely going to keep on trying to find the stolen puppies. But we all agreed that it was too important to have a missing man in our parish and to do nothing about it. We began to make a plan of action. Mark came up with the first really good idea. He said the police were bound to be doing everything that they could to find the missing man so he would ask his dad about the case. That was a really good idea because Mark's dad would just think that he was taking an interest in his work as The Look Outs are a secret club that only

Mark, Marion and I know about. That means that Mark's dad would have no idea that he was giving away initial clues.

Marion had become a real wiz at finding clues from taking photographs of the scene. A lot of people wouldn't take as much care as Marion, but we have found that the smallest detail that other people might overlook may become a really important clue as time goes on. Marion said that she would also ask to see Sister Bernadeen's newspaper at school. Just like she did when she was searching for information about the missing puppies.

Marion had lots of jobs at school. She does things like looking after the library and stuff like that. She reads Sister Bernadeen's paper quite often so there's no way that Sister Bernadeen would become suspicious. Next, we thought of a job for me. It was decided that I would get onto the Internet and find out any information which may become useful to us, just as Marion had done the day before. She said that I should try and find out anything about this case. She said that I might find out something about the case that wasn't in the newspapers. Mark said that his dad would know all of the information that wasn't in the newspapers and I agreed with him, but Marion said something really clever. She said that Mark's dad may know more about the case because he's a policeman but he may not tell Mark everything. She said that he may not be allowed to tell him everything because some things have to be kept secret. She said that Mark should try and have another sneaky look at his dad's notebook. We agreed that Marion was making sense, so we went over our jobs for the next day to make sure that we were absolutely clear about our tasks. Mark was also going to get his dad talking about the case to try and find out any inside information. Marion told Mark that he would have to make notes so that he could report back to The Look Outs, but Mark said that he couldn't sit in front of his dad making notes, because his dad would know that there was something funny going on. I agreed with Mark, but Marion said that notes were really important because vital clues or pieces of information could be forgotten or overlooked as time went by. Mark and I looked at each other and we knew that Marion was making sense. Mark said that he would go somewhere private and make some notes straight after he had spoken to his dad. I said that I would get on the Internet and find out as much as I could about this case and as much as I could about other cases where people had gone missing. Marion said that she would visit the missing man's house and take as many photographs as she could and then she would read Sister Bernadeen's newspaper. We all agreed to meet up at five o'clock the next day at The Look Outs den to report back with our findings.

As we were leaving to go home, I reminded the other two that we still had the case of the missing Golden Retriever puppies to think about. The other two promised that they would remember and we all went home.

Chapter Three – Danger in the Dark

Sometimes I walk to school by myself. My dad goes out to work early in the morning, so I normally get myself up. I make myself some tea and toast and then go off to school. Marion's mum and Mark's kind-of step mum normally walk to school with them. If I'm setting off around the same time, I'll walk with them. I walked with Mark and his kind-of step mum on the next morning because Marion had taken a different route to school. Marion told her mum that she wanted her article about the missing man to be really good. She asked her mum if they could walk past his house on the way to school so that she could take some photographs to put with her article in the school newspaper. Marion was really clever. She took the photograph for the St James Journal (that's what we call our school newspaper), but she also took plenty of photographs that may be helpful as clues.

School was brilliant at that time because we were putting on a school play. I had a little part in it. The play was about a princess who has to kiss a frog to turn him back into a prince. The problem was that the princess didn't know which one of the frogs was the prince, so she had to keep kissing frogs till she found the right one. You can guess who the princess was before I even tell. Yes, Marion was the princess. I was a butler who opened doors for her. Mark tried out for the play, but he fluffed his lines up a bit in the auditions, so they didn't give him a part. He was involved in it though.

Sister Bernadeen asked for volunteers to help in the making of the scenery, so the three of us said

that we would work together on it. We spent most of the day making some big trees. We cut the pattern of the tree out of cardboard and then we nailed some wood to the back of it so that we could make it stand up to form a backdrop to the play. Sister Bernadeen said that she wanted to take some photographs of our trees in the grounds of the convent because she wanted to use the photographs in the programme for the play. So she asked us if we could come to the convent at six o'clock to take the photographs. I said, "Yes" straight away because I can go where I want. Mark and Marion said that they would have to ask for permission at home time. We all wanted to go really badly. It's really great going to see Sister Bernadeen. She always makes homemade lemonade and cookies. There's only one thing in the whole world that is nicer than Sister Bernadeen's homemade lemonade and that is Sister Bernadeen's homemade cookies.

At home time, Marion and Mark asked for permission to go. Marion's mum said, "Yes" straight away, but Mark's kind-of step mum didn't seem keen on the idea. She said that she would be too busy to take him at that time. We said that we would go on our own, but she didn't like the sound of that at all. We told her that it was only two minutes away and that we only had to cross one little road. We could see that she was making her mind up. Then Marion's mum helped us out. She said that she would stand on the balcony outside of her flat and watch us cross the road. She said that she could see us nearly every inch of the way from there. That was good enough for Mark's kind-of step mum, so she let us go. The three of us hugged each other and we set off.

It was good fun making the scenery but we had Look Outs work to do as well. All that day, I had to keep on finding excuses to get onto the Internet so that I could find out more about people who go missing. Mark had to make notes about the information that he found out from his dad and Marion had to try and read Sister Bernadeen's newspaper. The Internet was really interesting. I found out the name of the man, where he lived and what his job was. But in truth, it was only information that we knew already from the news. The information that I found out about missing people in general was much more useful. The first thing was good news. Most people that go missing turn up safe and well within twenty four hours. Some people who go missing are not missing at all but simply fail to tell somebody where they are going. But sadly, it was true that some people go missing and they are never found again. I made up my mind to always tell somebody where I was. Mark made his notes and Marion got to read Sister Bernadeen's newspaper and she made lots of notes.

We walked home really quickly. Marion kept trying to get us to walk more quickly all of the time. I couldn't work out why she was so keen to get home because we weren't going to the old folks' home until after tea and we weren't holding a meeting of The Look Outs until after that. I asked Marion why she was in such a hurry, but she said that there was no reason. But I could tell that there was some reason. Then I realised what it was. She wanted to get home so that she could do her homework. Marion loves doing her homework. Mark and I do what we have to do, but we don't do anything we don't have to.

We met up after tea and went down to the old folks' home. Sister

Bernadeen was there to meet us. The old folks' home is called Nazareth House. Some nuns live there and they look after the old folks. We went down to the kitchen end of the old folks' home. There were some out buildings that were used in the olden days but nobody goes in them now. There's an old stable and a chain maker's shed. In the very, very olden days, there was a man who used to make chain by hand and that was his workplace. There are still some things from the olden days there, but they haven't been used for years. There's loads of dust and dirt in there and spiders' webs.

We were going to take the photograph just by the side of the chain maker's shed where there was a big garden with beautiful flowers and bushes. Sister Bernadeen gave us our trees and we held them in front of us and bent down behind them so that we could not be seen in the photograph. It was good fun and we knew what was coming next. Whenever we went to the old folks' home, we always had the same treat from Sister Bernadeen. She makes the homemade lemonade and cookies that I told you about, and they are seriously the best in the whole wide world. Sister Bernadeen phoned Mark's kind-of step mum to make sure that he was allowed some lemonade and cookies because he is a diabetic and he has to be careful what he eats. We ate the cookies and drank the lemonade and then we ran all of the way home so that we could hold a quick meeting of The Look Outs.

Mark knew that his kind-of step mum would call him to come in soon and that Marion would have to go in soon afterwards. So we got down to business really quickly. I told them about the details of the man and I told them how most people get found within twenty four hours and that some people are not really missing at all. Mark told us that his dad said that the man had recently lost his job and they think he might be really stressed and upset. Marion said that the newspaper never really had anything in it that Mark and I hadn't already found out. But she told us that she did have some good photographs of his house. Marion reached into her pocket to get her phone out and realised it was missing.

This was terrible. Not only had she lost her phone, but she had also lost her evidence as well. There was no time to lose. If we rushed back to the old folks' home, then we could find it and get back in just a few minutes. Marion said that it was a good idea and Mark agreed. We ran out of the shed and set off to run across to the old folks' home, but, as you know, we live in a block of flats and Mark's kind-of step mum and Marion's mum were out on the balcony looking for them. This meant that they had to go in.

I wasn't quite sure what I should do. I had permission to go to the old folks' home, so everyone would know I was there if anything happened to me, but it was starting to get dark. If I left it until the next day the phone may have gone and even if it was there, the photographs may be destroyed if it rained overnight. I decided to run down there quickly and then rush home. I was a bit scared. I had never really been out on my own after dark before.

I ran across our road and down by the side of the old folks' home. It's about a hundred metres to the entrance. I went inside and ran around by the side of the chapel and across the forecourt to the stables and the chain maker's shed and I began to look all around the places that we went to. I couldn't see any sign of the phone anywhere. I began to search the garden area when something startled me. I heard a car drive slowly around by the stable block. It was very odd, because there were no headlights to be seen. The engine was turned off and the car rolled down the last few metres slowly and silently. I hid behind one of the bushes and tried

to stop my breath from making too much noise. Two men got out of the car and hid down low and looked all around. They were dressed in black and they clearly didn't want anybody to know that they were there.

I was really frightened but I knew that if I made a sound they would hear me and they could do anything to me. I decided that I was going to run out and scream, "Sister Bernadeen! Sister Bernadeen!" at the top of my voice, but then I realised how stupid that was. Sister Bernadeen would almost certainly not hear me but the two men certainly would.

I decided to stay hidden behind the bush and stay very quiet. I was finding it very hard not to make too much noise with my breathing but I was so scared, I was finding it really hard to keep my breathing under control. To be honest, I was worried that my heart was beating so loudly that it might be enough to make the two men know I was there. One of the men pointed to a light that was on in one of the convent windows.

He whispered something to his partner, but I couldn't make out what it was. Then he pointed towards the chain maker's shed and the two of them started forwards. There was a big chain around the door. One of the men unlocked the chain. I could not see clearly enough to tell if he had a key or if he managed to pick the lock. I definitely wasn't going to put my head up above the bush for fear of being seen.

I could not for the life of me think why two men would want to sneak into an old abandoned shed. There was nothing in there worth stealing. I had looked in there that very evening. Everything in there was covered in layers of thick dust. There were only old anvils and chains that are no use to anybody anymore.

Once the two men were inside the shed, I realised that I had to try and make my escape. I stepped out from the bush and there on the ground in front of me was Marion's phone. I picked it up quickly and then stepped back behind the bush. I put it away in my pocket knowing that I couldn't waste anymore time. I had to escape now because staying where I was would be too risky. The two men could come out and see or hear me and I would be in deep trouble. I tiptoed forward and made my way across the garden to the side of the chain maker's shed. I thought about making a dash for it across the courtyard but the courtyard was made of gravel and it would make too much noise. I sneaked my way around the corner of the shed and peeped in through the window. I couldn't see much because the windows hadn't been cleaned in years. It was no use; the window was too small and too dirty for me to see anything so I took some more paces down to the next window which was a bit bigger. When I looked inside I couldn't believe what I was seeing. There was nobody there. The two men had vanished. There was no sign of them anywhere. I could see all around the room and they definitely weren't there. I couldn't see how they could just completely disappear into thin air. There was only one door and they definitely didn't come out of there. The only other thing that I could think of was that they may have climbed out of a rear window, but if they did that, I would surely have heard them. I decided that now wasn't the time to stand around and think about it. Now was the time to get out of there as fast as I could. I ran past the stable block and out through the gates and I didn't stop running until I got all the way back to the block of flats where we live.

I sent a text to Mark and told him to get Marion and meet me in the den. I told him that we needed to have an emergency meeting of The Look Outs. Mark knew that it must have been really important because I would never have called an emergency meeting if it were not really important. Mark went round to Marion's flat and asked her mum if she could come out. Marion's mum said that she was too busy doing her homework and it was too late for her to come out. Mark asked Marion's mum to pass on a message. He said, "Don't forget that your homework must say something about apples". That was really clever because apples is our key word. It is the secret sign that we give to each other if we need to hold a secret meeting of The Look Outs.

Mark came down to the den and in no time at all, Marion had joined us.

They thought that I had called the meeting just to talk about the phone, but they were shocked when I told them about the car rolling up with its lights off. Then they thought I was really brave when I told them about the way that I hid behind the bush and they just couldn't believe it when I told them how the two men had disappeared into thin air.

Marion put her hands behind her head and blew out a huge breath of air. We all sat in silence for a few moments

and wondered what kind of mystery we had gotten ourselves into.

Mark said that we couldn't do much now because his kind-of step mum would be calling him to come in and Marion said that her mum said she could only come out for five minutes. We agreed that we would come down early in the morning and hold a quick meeting before going off to school.

We all agreed to have a good think overnight about what would be our best plan of action.

Chapter Four – The Mystery Noise

I was the first person to get to the den. My dad goes out quite early to work in the morning. I get myself up. Sometimes I make a piece of toast for my breakfast, but today I was just too excited. I was sat on my own waiting for the other two for ages. I knew that it wasn't their fault that they couldn't get here as early as me. They get told to finish their breakfast and brush their teeth and they can't just go out when they want to.

When they did arrive, we got down to business really quickly. Their parents would be knocking on the door in no time telling us it was time to go to school. Mark had done something that I thought was absolutely brilliant. When his dad was snoozing on the settee, he sneaked his notebook from his uniform pocket. He hid down behind the settee and read through the notes as quickly as he could. His father had made a note about the stolen Golden Retriever puppies. He said that there had been reports that Golden Retriever puppies had been seen in a house near the Lickey Hills. That was really good news because we could get to the Lickey Hills in about ten minutes if we ran all the way. Marion said that we should find an excuse to be allowed to walk home on our own. Then we could take photographs which may become useful evidence. She said that we couldn't spend any more time talking about that, because we only had minutes before we would be told to leave. She asked if anybody had some good ideas about what we should do. Mark surprised us again. He said that we should tell Sister Bernadeen that we are interested to find out more about the history of the old folks' home. He said that if we got her talking about it, she may tell us something about the chain maker's shed that would help us solve the mystery of the two men sneaking around after dark. Before we could make any more decisions, Mark's phone beeped. It was a text from his kind-of step mum saying that she was leaving now so we had to meet at the front of the flats. I said that we hadn't decided how we were going to explain why we wanted to come home on our own. Marion told us to leave it to her. She was brilliant like that. She can make up lies faster than a heartbeat and everybody believes her.

We walked to school as usual, but Mark and I kept giving each other glances. We were worried that we were going to arrive at school before

Marion had found some way for us to come home on our own. Then she spoke. She asked her mum if we could run the rest of the way to school. Her mum said that of course we couldn't because she hadn't run in years. Then Marion said that we've been learning about stamina in P.E. and how we can build up stamina by running lots. Then Marion suggested that we could run home from school on our own. Her mum and Mark's kind-of step mum thought that would be a good idea. They said it would be a good idea for us to run more. I'm always amazed at how clever Marion is. She had sorted everything out. We would run home from school and by running as fast as we possibly could, we could go to the place where there had been a sighting of the Golden Retriever puppies. Now we had to get down to the other serious business of the day. We had to learn more about the mystery of the two men prowling about in the dark. More importantly, we needed to see if they had anything to do with the missing man.

I knew from my research on the Internet that it was really important to try and find a missing person as soon as possible. I spoke to Marion about this when we were lining up to go into class. Marion was as worried as me that we were running out of time. We were supposed to go down to assembly after registration, but Marion came up with a good idea. Our classroom was in a real mess because we had spent the previous day making scenery for the school play. So Marion asked Sister

Bernadeen if she could stay behind and tidy it up. Then she said, "Can Peter and Mark help me?" and Sister Bernadeen agreed. This was a great idea, because we could use the time to think about how we were going to find out about the history of the old folks' home.

As soon as everybody else had left the classroom, Marion gave me and Mark jobs to do. She said that we would have to talk and work at the same time.

As we tidied things away, we made plans for the day. I suggested that we just ask Sister Bernadeen to tell us about it, but Mark said that might make her suspicious. So Marion said that we could ask her how we could find out about local history. That seemed like a better idea because we were going to be learning all about local history, so she may think that it was normal for us to try and find out as much as we could.

When Sister Bernadeen and the rest of the class came back, we told her that we were interested in local history and she was really pleased.

She gave us some books to read and she said that we could spend some time looking through them. That was brilliant. It was just the breakthrough that we needed.

Sister Bernadeen gave us a pile of books to read and we went to the reading corner and started our research. There was a lot of stuff that was interesting but it wasn't really giving us the information that we wanted to know. We

live in Birmingham and some of the books told us how the city started and grew but that wasn't the kind of history that we wanted to know anything about. We wanted to know about the old folks' home and anything that might give us some clues about the chain maker's shed. We did find out some stuff about Longbridge that we thought may be useful. Longbridge is the area right opposite the old folks' home and there used to be a car factory there. It was all about Sir Herbert Austin who started the company. There was quite a lot about Sir Arthur Issigonis who designed the mini which was a famous car. We thought we might find something out about the old folks' home because it was so near but there was nothing there.

Then Mark found a book with a whole section about Nazareth House. That's what the old folks' home was called. Nazareth House used to be an orphanage where children 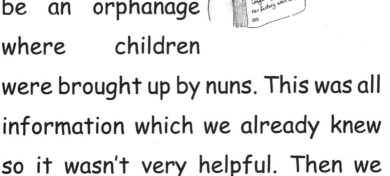 were brought up by nuns. This was all information which we already knew so it wasn't very helpful. Then we spotted a small section called The Chain Makers. This was the stuff which we thought could be really useful to us. There was a drawing of a chain maker with a hammer and a hot anvil. The book said that during most of the nineteenth century there were lots of small places where people made their own chains and nails, but they died out when factories started making them a hundred or even a thousand times more quickly than people could make them in a shed. It was all very interesting, but the truth is, we found nothing that may be of any use to us.

There was nothing else for it. We knew that we would have to investigate in person. We needed to find a reason to be at the old folks' home tonight after dark so that we could wait for the two men. That way, if they were connected to the missing man, we could catch them red handed and raise the alarm. We agreed to spend the rest of the day thinking of a reason why we should be at the old folks' home after dark.

The rest of the day was a slow torture. We hate having to sit through boring lessons when all that we really want to do is get on with the one thing we love more than anything else and that is 'Look Outs' business.

At the end of the school day, we still hadn't thought of a good reason to visit the old folks' home, but we couldn't wait around to talk about it because we had to run as fast as we could to the Lickey Hills. We couldn't even stop if we were out of breath because we were supposed to be running straight home from school. We set off at quite a pace and we just kept on running. We didn't even stop when we had a really steep hill in front of us. I'm the best runner so I was normally a little bit in front. Marion is normally the second best runner and Mark is just behind her, but sometimes he can beat Marion.

We got to the house where the Golden Retrievers had been spotted but we couldn't see or hear anything. We sneaked around the back of the house and looked inside a crack in the fence but we found nothing. We couldn't spend any more time there because Marion and Mark would get into trouble if we didn't get home soon and we still hadn't found a good reason to go to the old folks' home after dark. We looked at each other for a while. We just couldn't think of anything to say. Mark said that we were trying to do too much. He said that we should stick to one case at a time in future. I knew what he meant. We could hardly give all of our attention to the case of the stolen Golden Retriever puppies and give our full attention to the case of the missing man at the same time. Then a really good idea came into my head. The last time that I was there after dark I was looking for Marion's phone. This time we could say that we were looking for my phone. The other two thought that was a brilliant idea. We ran home without stopping and agreed that I would call for them after tea.

I sent texts to both Marion and Mark asking them if they were going to be allowed to come down to the old folks' home with me. They each sent texts back saying that they were working on it. They both had to virtually beg for permission. They had to promise to phone home as soon as they got there and they also had to promise that they wouldn't stay too late, but eventually, they both got permission.

It had already gone dark by the time that I called for Marion and Mark and in no time, we found ourselves hiding in the bushes waiting to see if the two men returned. We were whispering to each other quite freely because there was no sign of the two men. Suddenly Mark told us to be quiet. He said that he had heard something. Marion and I listened but we couldn't hear anything. We thought that Mark was hearing things. But he made us listen some more. Then we realised that he was right. We could hear something. It was a kind of crying noise and it was coming from the chain maker's shed. We went to the window to look in, but everything was exactly the same as it always was. Nothing had been moved. The windows were really dirty, but not so dirty as to stop us being able to look all around the room. There was no hiding place at all. If the missing man was there then he must be invisible because there was no sign of him.

Then we heard a car pull in through the gates and we darted back behind the bushes to wait in safety. The car lights were turned off, just like the night before and the driver also turned the engine off so as not to make any noise as he rolled towards the courtyard and the chain maker's shed. This was our time. This was the moment that we were set to find out if the two dodgy looking men had anything to do with the case of the missing man.

As the car came to a standstill, Mark said that they might have the man tied up in the boot. I said that we should use our phones to get help or run and shout for Sister Bernadeen, but Marion said that we should stand still for a few moments and see what they do. The two men got out of the car just as they had done the night before. They looked all around to make sure that they hadn't been spotted. Then they crept to the door of the chain maker's shed. I could see a little bit better tonight and it was clear that one of them had a key. Once the two men were inside, we slowly made our way down to peer in through the window. Then we saw what the two men were

up to. They lifted a hatch and bought a ladder down. Then they climbed up the ladder to a loft. We had no idea it was there. That must be where they were keeping the missing man.

Marion is always clever. I'm used to her doing clever things, but sometimes she amazes me by being fiercely brave as well. She climbed down below the window and crept towards the door. She took the chain which had been left on the floor and she used it to lock the door up. Then

she ran to the car and took the keys from the ignition. Then she pointed back towards the hiding place and we all ran back behind the bush. Marion got her phone out and said that her and Mark should phone their parents and tell them to come at once. She told Mark to tell his dad to bring some other police officers with him to arrest some criminals. She told me to run and tell Sister Bernadeen and the caretaker, but I said that we didn't know that they were criminals. We didn't know that the missing man was even in there. Marion said that they must be criminals because only criminals would turn their lights and engine off and only criminals would skulk around late at night trying to make sure that nobody was watching. So we agreed that we should raise the alarm even if the missing man wasn't in there. I went into the old folks' home and the others called their parents.

In no time at all, the quiet and the dark of the courtyard was filled with light. The lights went on all around the old folks' home and police cars came driving up the path. We told Mark's dad all about the mystery men and how they turned their lights and engine off. I told them that they had done exactly the same thing the night before. Marion gave me a fierce look. I knew that I had said too much but I was so excited I couldn't stop myself. Mark's dad asked me why I was there last night and I explained that I was there because Marion had lost her phone.

Then he asked me why I was there tonight and I said that tonight I had lost my phone. Mark's dad said that we might have to have a little talk about that, but for now he said that he would have to sort these two men out.

Mark's dad pulled the chain from the door and told the two men to come down because they were surrounded by police. Sister Bernadeen took the three of us to a safe distance and Marion's mum came and stood with us. The two men could see all of the lights outside and they knew that they had been caught. The two men came down and Mark's dad told them to put their hands behind their heads and then he handcuffed them and led them away.

We told Mark's dad that the missing man was in the loft but he said that he didn't think that he was. We told him that we had heard sounds which sounded like a man crying in the loft. But Mark's dad told us that the missing man had been found. He was safe and well and staying at a friend's house. So we asked him who it was that was making the noise and he said he would find out. Mark's dad made us stay back. He went into the shed and climbed the steps to the loft.

We never imagined in our wildest dreams what was hidden up there. A few moments later Mark's dad emerged from the shed with a little Golden Retriever puppy in each arm.

They were beautiful. He gave them to us to hold and then went back into the shed. He said there were a few more up there. A minute later he came back out with more puppies.

The two thieves had been very busy indeed. They had been stealing pedigree puppies to order. They had a nice little business going. They found people who wanted puppies and then went out and stole them. Their business was worth hundreds, even thousands of pounds. Sister Bernadeen told us all to come inside and to get the puppies in out of the cold.

Chapter Five – Snuggles

We moved into Sister Bernadeen's living room and put the puppies down on the carpet in front of the fire. It turned out one of the thieves used to be an odd job man at the old folks' home so he knew where the hiding place was. The thieves had been very cruel indeed. They had kept the puppies locked up in the loft and had planned to keep them there for a few weeks so that the people they were selling them to would not suspect that they were the stolen puppies. The worst thing that they did was to tape up the dogs mouths so that they couldn't bark. Each evening they had been coming in to give them some food and some drink. The poor puppies were shivering and cold but they were wagging their tails now that we had them in the warm and were looking after them.

Mark's dad said that they had been searching all over the place for where the puppies may have been locked away. They knew that they couldn't have been sold whilst they were all over the newspapers and the T.V. but the thieves had been very clever in finding somewhere like the chain maker's shed because they could go there every day to feed them without anybody knowing. But then he said that they never bargained for three young children to be snooping around.

The adults all looked at us waiting for an explanation. Sister Bernadeen said that we could give the explanation in a few minutes. She said that the adults needed a nice cup of tea and the children needed a nice treat. We all knew what she meant by a nice treat. You know already without me even having to tell you. Sister Bernadeen makes the most beautiful homemade lemonade in the whole wide world and when she gives us some, she also gives us some of her beautiful home made cookies as well.

When Sister Bernadeen went to prepare the drinks, the three of us sat on the carpet in front of the fire and played with the puppies. Marion and Mark just gently stroked the puppies

because they were still a bit frightened. I could play properly with one puppy because he kept on coming to me and snuggling up. He kept on jumping onto my lap and trying to lick my face.

I could tell that the parents were a little bit cross with us because they wanted to know what we had been up to. But one of the puppies did a wee on the carpet and everybody laughed. Then Sister Bernadeen came in with the drinks. The adults drank their tea and we got stuck into the homemade lemonade and cookies. Marion's mum asked for the recipe from Sister Bernadeen but Sister Bernadeen said that it was a secret that she was going to keep for the rest of her life and all of the adults laughed.

Once everybody had a drink, Mark's dad said, "Come on then you three. I think you've got some explaining to do. I suspect that you've been up to your detective club thing again haven't you?"

I looked down at the puppy I was playing with and Mark drew a circle in the carpet with his finger. Then Marion said she could explain what we had been doing. She said that we had been working as 'The Look Outs' and we had seen some men acting suspiciously so we decided to see if they came back tonight so that we could let everybody know.

The adults seemed to think that was reasonable enough because they knew where we were at all times and Sister Bernadeen was nearby. Then the owner of the puppies turned up and put a beautiful bright green collar down on the side. It had sparkling studs on it and it looked very posh indeed. He went over and patted the puppies on the head and stroked them. He seemed to be very impressed by the way my puppy wouldn't let me go. He told me that I appeared to have a new best friend. I agreed with him. I thought that the little puppy snuggling up to me really did want to be my new best friend. He kept snuggling his head into my chest and trying to lick my face. The owner told us that his dog was really upset because her puppies had been taken away from her too soon. He had brought her to see the puppies. When she came in they all ran towards her. All except one and that was the one that was snuggling up to me.

Mark's dad phoned my dad and told him everything that had happened. Then he passed the phone to me. I told my dad that I had a puppy who was my new best friend because he would not let me go and he kept snuggling up to me. Without thinking I just said, "Can I keep him dad? Can I keep him?" And I had the biggest shock in the world when my dad said yes! He said that if the owner didn't mind then I could keep him. I asked the owner and he said he supposed I deserved him because they never would have found him if it weren't for me and my two friends. I couldn't

believe it. I held the puppy close to my cheek and then I jumped up and down around the room. Then Mark and Marion joined me and we were all jumping up and down and screaming and shouting. Then the dogs started barking and the adults were laughing. My puppy wouldn't stop licking my face no matter how much I tried to pull away. It was the best night of my entire life. Nothing as wonderful as this had ever happened to me before.

Mark's dad said that we had better get off before we woke up every old person in the house. Sister Bernadeen stroked my puppy and then she patted me on the head. She told me that it was a big responsibility to look after a dog and that I had to make sure he had plenty of exercise. I promised her that no dog in the world would be better looked after than my little dog.

We all walked down the big corridor towards the door and I told everyone that I had left my phone on the side. Mark's dad said that I kept losing my phone a lot lately and everybody laughed. I quickly ran back to the room and caught up with everybody before they were even outside the building. I carried my little puppy all the way home because he was too small to walk on his own. When we reached the block of flats where we lived, Mark and Marion stroked my puppy and said goodnight. We all agreed that we would have a lot to tell our friends when we got to school in the morning.

Normally Mark and Marion went back to their homes with their family and I went home to be by myself because there's only me and my dad and he is out most of the time, but not anymore. I won't be lonely ever again, not now that I have my new best friend to snuggle up to me.

I went straight up to bed and put my little puppy at the bottom of the bed to settle down to sleep. He never stayed there though, he ran up the bed so that he could snuggle

up close to me.
He makes me
laugh because
all he wants to
do is snuggle up
close and lick
my face and
my neck. I sat
up in bed and

stroked him some more. "Snuggle, snuggle, snuggle" I said. "All you want to do is snuggle." That's it, I thought to myself. I would call him Snuggles. I lay back down in bed and I promised him that I would teach him to do more things than any other dog in the world. I told him that I would take him everywhere that I go. I even told him that if Mark and Marion didn't mind he could become a member of The Look Outs.

I lay in bed thinking about the adventures that I had enjoyed during the last couple of days. I thought about the way we ran to the Lickey Hills, I thought about how frightened I was when I was hiding behind the bushes and the two men arrived with their car lights and their engine turned off. I thought how wonderful life was going to be now that I had Snuggles to share everything with me. Best of all, I would never be lonely again. Snuggles buried his whole body up close to me and I could feel his heart beating.

I heard my phone buzz which was very unusual because Marion and Mark weren't allowed to use their phones at night. It was Mark. He text me to ask if I saw what had happened to the nice collar and lead that the owner of the puppies had put on the side. I knew the one he meant and I text back to say that I knew nothing about it. I did though. I stole it. When I went back to Sister Bernadeen's living room, I said I was going back to get my phone. I wasn't though. I went back to steal the collar and lead. It was a bit big for Snuggles, so I just left it on the side in my room. I know it's wrong to steal but I can't stop myself. It's so much fun and I enjoy it so much. But I do know that it's wrong and I am going to stop it. I did tell you at the start of this story that I was a thief, didn't I?

I lay in bed and imagined myself training Snuggles to do lots of fabulous tricks. I thought how funny it would be if I had called him 'Sit Down'. If I did that, I would have to teach him to sit down by giving him a different command. Maybe I could tell him to stand up when I wanted him to sit down. Maybe if I wanted him to stand up I could say fetch. But then I would have to think of something else for fetch. So if I wanted him to come and sit down and stand by my side I would have to say, "Here Sit Down. Sit Down stand up. Stand up Sit Down and fetch." It was all a bit silly and I am glad that I called him Snuggles. Sometimes I wanted to call him Snuggle and sometimes I wanted to call him Snuggles. I suppose it wouldn't matter. I'm sure he would answer to both. I became so tired that I drifted off to sleep. Even the most exciting day of your life has to come to an end sometime and I couldn't stop myself going to sleep.

Other titles by E. R. Reilly

Harriet the Horrible
Best Friends
Rashnu
Tall Tales
Gnome Alone
One Boy, One Club, One Dream
The Amazing Time Travelling Adventures of
Professor McGinty in Ancient Greece
The Look Outs
The Children's Lottery

Contact us at

SANTIAGO PRESS

PO BOX 8808

BIRMINGHAM

B30 2LR

santiago@reilly19.freeserve.co.uk

Visit the website at www.er-reilly.co.uk.